Adapted by Diane Molleson
Based on the screenplay by
Susan Gauthier and Bruce Graham
Illustrated by Brad McMahon

A 20th Century Fox Presentation

ANASTASIA

A Don Bluth/Gary Goldman Film

My Anastasia
Storybook & Necklace

HarperActive™
A Division of HarperCollinsPublishers

St. Petersburg, Russia
About eighty years ago

Anastasia Romanov was the youngest daughter of Nicholas II, the Czar of Imperial Russia. She lived happily with her family until one cold winter evening, when her life changed forever.

On the three hundredth anniversary of their family's rule, Princess Anastasia and her family celebrated with a grand ball. That night, Anastasia's grandmother, the Dowager Empress Marie, gave her a special music box that played Anastasia's favorite lullaby.

"You can play it before you go to sleep. And pretend it's me singing," the Empress told Anastasia.

Anastasia clutched the music box to her chest. She knew her grandmother would be leaving soon to return to Paris, and she always missed her very much.

Then Anastasia's grandmother handed her a gold flower-shaped key that opened the music box. The key hung on a necklace. "Read what the key says."

"'Together in Paris,'" Anastasia read out loud. "Really? Oh, Grandmama." Carefully, Anastasia fastened the necklace around her neck.

Suddenly, the crowd gasped at the sight of a

man dressed in black. On the man's shoulder rode a small, white bat, and he wore a glowing reliquary on a cord around his waist. He stepped right up to Nicholas II. "You think you can banish the great Rasputin," he said angrily. "It is I who will destroy you. I will not rest until I see the end of the Romanov line forever."

In the blink of an eye, bricks smashed through one of the palace windows and a mob of angry soldiers and workers stormed the palace. A servant boy named Dimitri helped Anastasia and her grandmother escape through a secret door hidden in a wall.

Anastasia and her grandmother fled from the palace across a frozen river. To her horror, Anastasia saw that Rasputin was chasing them. "You'll never escape me, child. Never!" he cried, as he grabbed Anastasia's ankle.

But just as Rasputin said those words, the ice broke beneath him, and he fell into the river. All that was left of the evil magician was his reliquary, which the bat carried away.

Anastasia and her grandmother ran and ran. When they reached the train station, hundreds of people were shoving to board a train. As they tried to get on, Anastasia and her grandmother became separated. Anastasia fell and bumped her head, just as the train began to move. On board, the Empress wondered if she would ever see her beloved granddaughter again.

Ten years later

An eighteen-year-old girl, dressed in rags, stood outside an orphanage talking to the headmistress.

"I got you a job in the fish factory," said the headmistress. "Are you listening, Anya?"

"I'm listening," answered the orphan as she fingered her necklace.

The headmistress sighed. Anya always seemed more interested in her necklace than in anything else. She leaned toward Anya and peered at the necklace. "'Together in Paris,'" the headmistress read. "So you want to go to France to find your family, huh?"

Anya nodded. The headmistress laughed rudely. "Little Miss Anya, it's time to take your place in life. And be grateful, too."

Anya started down the road. "I am grateful," she muttered. "Grateful to get away." Anya had lived at the orphanage for ten years, ever since she had been found wandering the streets of St. Petersburg unable to remember who she was.

Soon Anya came to a fork in the road. She had two choices: She could go to St. Petersburg and try to find a way to get to Paris, or she could work in a fish factory the rest of her days.

Anya looked up at the sky. "Send me a sign, a hint, anything," she prayed.

A puppy ran up to Anya and grabbed her scarf.

"I don't have time to play with you. I'm waiting for a sign," said Anya. The puppy ran up the road to St. Petersburg.

"Oh, great. A puppy wants me to go to St. Petersburg. Okay."

When Anya reached St. Petersburg, the agent at the train station said, "No exit visa, no ticket."

"Oh no! What am I going to do?" said Anya.

"Psst—see Dimitri," whispered a woman who was sweeping the station. "You can find him at the old palace."

Anya and her puppy, whom she had named Pooka, reached the royal palace just as the sun was setting.

"Hello? Anybody home?" Anya called as she entered.

The palace looked huge and very empty. Broken windows rattled with the wind, and torn tapestries hung on the walls.

Anya walked toward a large vase painted with dancing bears, then looked at the portraits of the Romanov family. "This place—it's like a memory from a dream."

"Hey!" A man's voice interrupted Anya's day-dream. "What are you doing in here?" The voice belonged to Dimitri, who used to be a servant in the palace. Now he lived here with his friend Vladimir, and the two made their living selling the forgotten treasures.

When Anya turned toward Dimitri, he gulped. "Vlad, do you see what I see?" he asked his friend.

Vladimir clapped his hands together. "Yes, yes," he said. Anya looked just like the Princess Anastasia in the Romanov family portrait! Dimitri and Vladimir had been searching all over St. Petersburg for an Anastasia look-alike, and here she was standing before them.

"Are you Dimitri?" asked Anya.

"It depends on who's looking for him."

"My name is Anya. I need travel papers. They say you're the man to see."

Dimitri smiled. He said, "Let me ask you something—Anya, was it? Is there a last name that goes with that?"

"I don't know my last name," answered Anya. "I have very few memories of my past. But I do have one clue. Paris."

"Paris," said Dimitri.

"So can you two help me with my travel papers?"

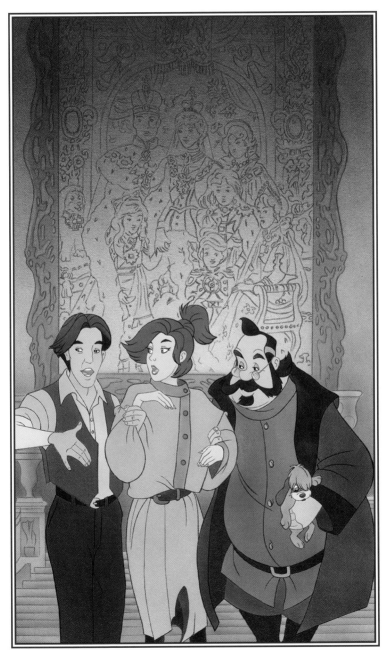

"Ah," said Dimitri. "I've got three tickets right here. Unfortunately, the third one is for Anastasia."

"Anastasia who?" asked Anya.

"Romanov!" Dimitri answered. How could Anya not know of Anastasia Romanov? All of St. Petersburg was talking about her. They were saying she might still be alive. And her grandmother, the Empress, would pay a big reward to anyone who found her. Dimitri and Vladimir wanted that money.

"You know, you do kind of resemble Anastasia," said Dimitri.

"Are you trying to tell me that I could be royalty? Me? Anastasia?" asked Anya.

Dimitri and Vladimir nodded.

"I don't remember who I am. Who's to say I'm not a princess or a duchess? I guess I could be Anastasia," said Anya. "And if I'm not Anastasia, the Empress will certainly know right away."

Dimitri nodded.

"But if you *are* the Princess," added Vladimir, "you'll finally know who you are and have your family back."

Dimitri laughed. "Either way, it gets you to Paris," he said.

"Oh, Pooka, we're going to Paris," said Anya.

High in the rafters of the palace lived a white bat named Bartok. He had never paid much attention to Dimitri and Vladimir. But he did tonight. He could not believe he was looking down at the real Anastasia Romanov. He knew it must be she, because Rasputin's reliquary was glowing.

Suddenly the reliquary took off like a rocket, taking Bartok with it. "Whoa!" screamed Bartok. It dragged him into the icy river and traveled far down through the mud under the water. At last they reached Rasputin's chamber.

"Who dares intrude?" cried Rasputin. "This is my private hell. Get out!"

"Ahh, ooh . . . Master? You're alive?"

"Bartok, is that you? I am alive in a manner of speaking," answered Rasputin, as one of his eyeballs popped out. "What's happened, Bartok?"

Bartok gulped. "I saw her—Anastasia," he told his master.

"That Romanov brat! That's why I'm stuck here in limbo! My curse is unfulfilled. If only I hadn't lost the key to my powers."

"You mean this?" said Bartok, showing Rasputin the reliquary.

"Where did you get that? Give it to me!" cried Rasputin. "I swear this time I will not fail." The reliquary glowed even more brightly as hundreds of horrible minions flew out of it.

Anya, Dimitri, Vladimir, and Pooka settled into their train compartment, unaware of the danger ahead.

That night, Rasputin sent his minions to destroy the train. The minions set the engine on fire. The train car carrying Anya and the others went out of control and almost crashed. But thanks to quick thinking by Anya and Dimitri, they were all able to jump to safety. They landed in a large snowbank.

Bartok had never seen his master so angry. "How could they let her escape?" Rasputin screamed.

"It's very upsetting, sir," said Bartok. He picked up the reliquary and threw it over his shoulder. "I guess this thing's broken," he added.

"You idiot!" Rasputin sputtered. He caught the reliquary in midair and shoved it under Bartok's nose. "I sold a piece of myself to harness this power. To destroy the Romanovs. If those demons escape, they'll come for the rest of me. I need to do something really fiendish. . . ."

Meanwhile, Anya, Pooka, Dimitri, and Vladimir had to walk for days to reach a port where they could get on a ship bound for France. As they walked, Vladimir hummed and kept repeating the name Sophie.

"Who's Sophie?" Anya finally asked.

"She is the Dowager Empress's ravishing first cousin," answered Vladimir.

"Nobody gets near the Dowager Empress without convincing Sophie first," said Dimitri.

Dimitri and Vladimir had known their share of royalty. They taught Anya how to walk, talk, and act like a princess. They made her memorize

the names of all the Russian royalty, what they liked to eat, what they wore, and where they went for their vacations. Anya's head was spinning, but she learned.

When they reached the ship, Dimitri gave Anya a present—a new dress. Anya put it on, and she looked just like a real princess.

"Now that you are dressed for a ball, you will learn to dance at one," said Vladimir. "Dimitri, dance with Anya."

"But I'm not very good," protested Dimitri.

"*One*-two-three. *One*-two-three," counted Vladimir as Anya and Dimitri began to dance.

"That dress is really beautiful," Dimitri whispered to Anya. Anya smiled back at him.

When the dance was over, Vladimir looked at them and shook his head. He could tell they were in love.

That night, as Anya slept in her cabin, Rasputin sent her a nightmare. Sleepwalking, Anya went up on deck. She dreamed she saw a family swimming in a beautiful pool. Just as Anya was about to leap in to join them, she saw the face of a horrible creature. "Jump!" it ordered.

Suddenly Dimitri ran onto the deck. "Anya, no, no!" he cried as he grabbed her around the waist.

Startled, Anya awoke from her dream. She looked down at the churning water and then threw her arms around Dimitri, sobbing. "The Romanov curse . . . I keep seeing faces."

"It was a nightmare. You're safe now," said Dimitri.

"No, no!" screamed Rasputin when his reliquary showed him that Anya was still alive. Rasputin was so upset, he pounded his fist on the wall. His hand flew across the room.

"Take it easy, Master," said Bartok.

Rasputin took a deep breath. "You're right. I

am calm. I am heartless. I have no feelings whatsoever. I'll just have to kill her myself."

When Anya, Dimitri, and Vladimir arrived in Paris, Vladimir led them straight to Sophie's door. "Come in, come in, everyone," said Sophie. She looked delighted to see Vladimir, who lost no time in introducing Anya.

"Heavens, she does look like Anastasia," said Sophie. "But so did so many of the others."

"How did you escape during the siege of the palace?" Sophie asked Anya.

Vladimir and Dimitri looked at one another. They had not prepared Anya for that question.

"There was a boy, a boy who worked in the palace. He opened the wall—I'm sorry. That's crazy—walls opening," said Anya.

Dimitri stared at Anya. He was the servant boy who had helped Princess Anastasia escape. He now knew Anya was the real Anastasia—and he was shocked.

Sophie asked Anya many more questions, and Anya answered every one. But unfortunately, Sophie told them, the Empress did not want to see any more girls claiming to be Anastasia.

"Please," Vladimir pleaded.

Finally she agreed they could meet the Empress that very night at the ballet.

That evening, Vladimir and Dimitri paced in front of the Paris Opera House waiting for Anya.

"We have nothing to be nervous about," said Dimitri. "I was the boy in the palace—the one who opened the secret door in the wall. She's the real thing."

Vladimir could not believe it. "That means our Anya has found her family. We have found the heir to the Russian throne. And you . . ." He looked sadly at his friend.

". . . will walk out of her life forever. But we're going through with this as if nothing has changed," said Dimitri.

Dimitri gasped when Anya arrived. He had never seen her look more beautiful.

At intermission, Dimitri and Anya headed for the Empress's private box. Unfortunately, Dimitri could not convince the Empress that he had found the real Anastasia. She summoned a guard, who threw Dimitri out of her private box. He landed at Anya's feet.

Anya had overheard the whole conversation and was heartbroken. "It was all a lie, wasn't it?" she asked. "I was just part of your con to get her money."

"No!" Dimitri insisted. "Look, it may have started out that way, but everything's different now, because you really *are* Anastasia."

"Just leave me alone!" Anya shouted as she turned and ran off through the crowd.

Dimitri knew of only one way he could make the Empress believe him—with the music box she had given Anastasia ten years before. Luckily, Dimitri had rescued the music box from the palace and brought it with him from St. Petersburg. When he burst back in and showed it to the Empress, she clutched it to her chest.

That evening, the Empress knocked on Anya's door.

"Go away, Dimitri," said Anya crossly. She was still angry at him.

The door opened softly. Anya spun around and saw the Empress for the first time. "Oh, I'm sorry. I thought you were..." As the Empress walked by, Anya caught a scent of her perfume.

"Peppermint?" Anya asked.

The Empress looked suspicious. "An oil for my hands."

Anya closed her eyes. She began to remember. "Yes, I spilled a bottle. The carpet was soaked, and it forever smelled of peppermint. Like you!"

The Empress Marie stared, dumbfounded, at Anya. Of all the fake Anastasias she had seen, Anya was the best actress by far. She noticed Anya playing with her necklace. "What is that?" asked the Empress.

"This? Well, I've always had it, ever since before I can remember."

"May I?" asked the Empress, reaching for the key. Anya handed it to her.

The Empress looked at the key for a long time. Then she reached inside her handbag for the music box. She began to cry softly. "It was our secret. My Anastasia's and mine."

Anya gently took the key from the Empress and put it in the box. She remembered how the music box worked, how much she had missed her grandmother every time she went to Paris, how much she had loved her whole family.

"Anastasia! My Anastasia," cried the Empress as she embraced her. She had found her granddaughter at last.

The following morning, Dimitri refused to accept the Empress's reward. The Empress looked puzzled. "You were the boy, weren't you? The servant boy who got us out. You saved her life and mine. Then you restored her to me, yet you want no reward?"

Dimitri shook his head. "I must go," he said.

That night, the Empress gave a grand ball to welcome Anastasia. Anastasia wore a beautiful gown and a crown on her head. She watched the dancing couples and wondered where Dimitri was.

"There are so many people," said Anastasia to her grandmother.

"He's not there," said the Empress.

"Who's not there, Grandmama?" Anastasia asked, pretending not to know what she was talking about.

The Empress looked fondly at Anastasia. She knew Anastasia had been searching for Dimitri. "The young man who found the music box," she said.

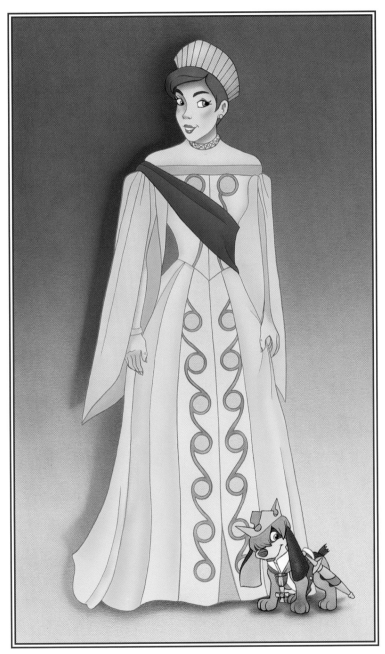

"He's too busy spending his reward money as fast as he can," said Anastasia.

"He didn't take the money," said the Empress.

Anastasia looked at her in disbelief. She had thought the money was all Dimitri ever wanted.

"You will have to decide what to do, my darling. There is no place for him out there in that glittering crowd, no place for him beside the Grand Duchess Anastasia," said the Empress as she kissed Anastasia's forehead. "Whatever you choose, I will hold you in my heart always."

A moment later, Anastasia heard Pooka barking. Then he disappeared through the terrace doors that opened onto the garden.

Anastasia went outside to look for him. When Pooka didn't answer her call, Anastasia searched the

garden, then walked out onto a bridge that crossed a large river.

"An-a-sta-sia," a voice called.

A dark figure appeared in the moonlight. "Your Imperial Highness," it said. "Look what ten years have done to us: you a beautiful flower and me a rotting corpse."

The figure raised his reliquary, and a blast of light exploded at Anastasia's feet.

"Rasputin!" Anastasia cried out. All at once, she remembered everything.

Rasputin laughed triumphantly as his minions swarmed around Anastasia, pushing her toward the edge of the bridge.

"I'm not afraid of you," Anastasia said bravely.

Suddenly Dimitri appeared and tackled Rasputin. Then Pooka leaped up and grabbed the reliquary, dropping it at Anastasia's feet. Furiously, she stomped on it, smashing it to bits!

Rasputin screamed in agony as thousands of minions surrounded him and destroyed him—forever!

Later that evening, at the grand ball, the butler handed the Empress a package. Inside, she found Anastasia's crown and a note. Anastasia was not coming back. She had decided to spend the rest of her life with Dimitri.

Sophie wiped her eyes. "It seems like only yesterday she came here!" she said.

"At least we had that yesterday," the Empress replied. "Now she has her tomorrow."

Meanwhile, Anastasia and Dimitri embraced under a starry sky. Pooka barked happily. He knew they had found their home at last—with each other.